All That Glitters

By Lara Bergen

ILLUSTRATED BY the Disney Storybook Artists

Disney PRESS

New York

Printed in the United States of America

First Edition

1 3 5 7 9 10 8 6 4 2

G942-9090-6-09288

Library of Congress Catalog Card Number on file.

ISBN 978-1-4231-3017-8

For more Disney Press fun, visit www.disneybooks.com

SUSTAINABLE FORESTRY INITIATIVE

Certified Fiber Sourcing

www.sfiprogram.org

PWC-SFICOC-260

Table of Contents

Ariel
and the Aquamarine Jewel

*I*t was a glorious summer morning—a perfect day, thought Ariel, for a walk along the shore. Happily, she set out, and soon enough her friend Scuttle the seagull joined her.

The two friends were far down the beach when Ariel's foot struck something hard in the sand.

"Ouch! My toes!" she cried, still not entirely used to the feel of human feet. She looked down, surprised to see something gleaming in the sand. She dug it out and pulled off a layer of seaweed. She slowly turned the shiny object over in her hand.

"Whatcha got there, Princess?" Scuttle asked. "Looks like a piece of that sweet gnobblybloop you humans like so much. Yum! Can I have a taste?" And with that, he stuck out his tongue and licked it! "Blagh!" he exclaimed.

Ariel laughed. "I think you mean 'candy,'" she told her friend. "And no, I don't think it's that. I think it's a *jewel*!" she cried.

But where had it come from? Ariel wondered. She'd never seen anything like it in the kingdom before. Perhaps it had come from the sea! And if so, she knew just whom to ask about it.

"Scuttle," she said quickly, "please go find Sebastian. Ask him to get my father right away!"

A short while later, Ariel's father, King
Triton, emerged from beneath the waves.

"Ariel, my dear," declared the king,
"Sebastian said you called."

"Yes, Father," said Ariel. "You see,
I found this lovely jewel on the shore.
Do you know where it came from?"

King Triton looked at her sadly. "Indeed, I do. In fact," said the king, "I'll show you. But I'll have to change you back into a mermaid to do it."

And with a blast from his mighty trident, that's exactly what he did!

Gripping the water-colored jewel, Ariel dove
into the sea. She'd nearly forgotten how wonderful
it felt to swim freely through the water! By the
time she and King Triton reached Atlantica, she
felt very comfortable. It was as if she'd never left.

"Why, Father," Ariel cried excitedly, "this jewel
is from Atlantica?"

Ariel's excitement faded, however, when her father led her to his throne room. "It looks like a tidal wave's been through here!" she said with a gasp. "And Atlantica's treasure—it's gone!"

"Alas," King Triton said, "it's true. This chest has kept our kingdom's treasures safe for years. And then one giant wave comes and washes them all away! That aquamarine is just one of many gems that were lost."

"Don't worry, Father," said Ariel. "I'll help you find the other jewels! After all, I'm a pretty good treasure hunter."

First, Ariel decided to search the old sunken ship—a place she still knew like the back of her fin. In and out of the galleon she swam, until she had found close to a dozen of the missing jewels!

Next, it was off to the coral reef, where it was easy to understand how jewels could be overlooked among all the deep crevasses and bright colors. But with a little help from Flounder and some other dear old friends, yet more lost jewels were found.

By the time the tide turned, Atlantica's treasure chest was full again.

"Ariel, on behalf of Atlantica, I thank you," said King Triton.

"I'm just glad all the jewels are back where they belong," she replied.

The king thought for a moment. "Actually," he said, "I'm not sure that they are all where they belong." He reached into the treasure chest and pulled out the first, and by far the most beautiful, aquamarine that Ariel had found.

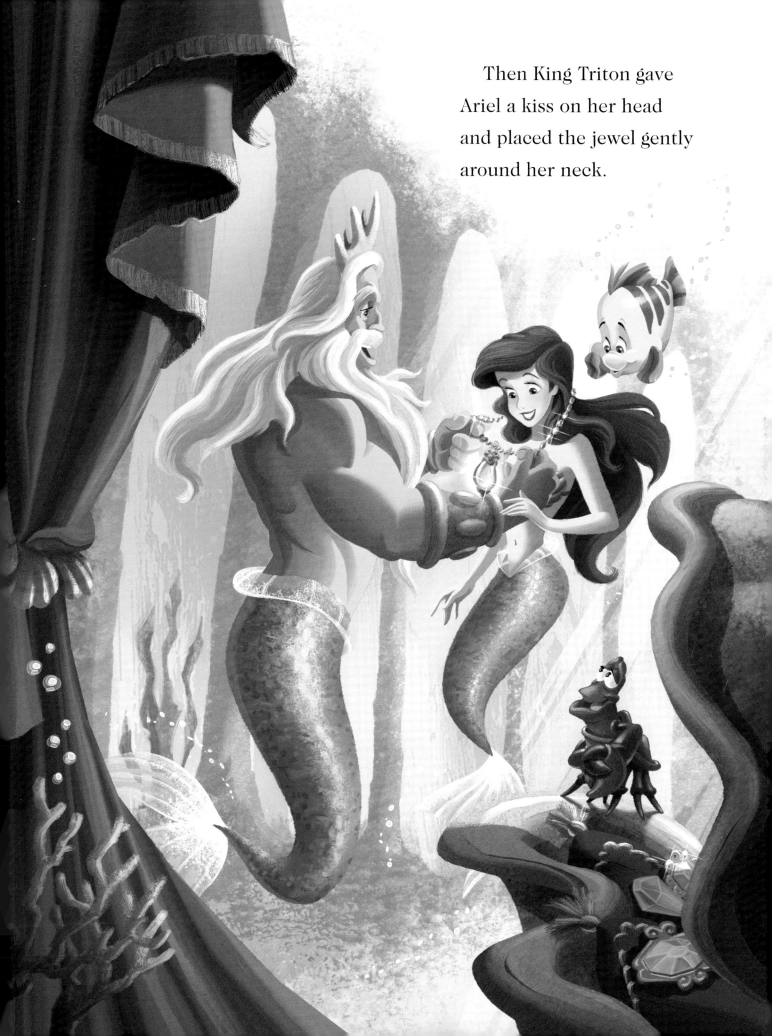

Then King Triton gave
Ariel a kiss on her head
and placed the jewel gently
around her neck.

It was now time, they both knew, for
Ariel to swim back to her own castle and
become a human princess once again.

That night, Ariel told Prince Eric all about her adventure. As she did, she touched the aquamarine jewel and gazed out across the sea. Though she knew that her father was never far away, it still felt good to have a piece of Atlantica with her always.

Aurora

and the Diamond Crown

Aurora awoke one sunny morning in the most cheerful of moods. It was her seventeenth birthday, and she could not wait to see what wonderful surprises were in store.

As soon as Aurora had gotten dressed, her mother, the
Queen, came in wearing a crown Aurora had never seen before.
Gleaming at its center was a large, pink, heart-shaped diamond
trimmed all around with tiny, sparkling diamonds.

"Mother!" she cried. "What a beautiful crown! Is it new?"

"Actually," replied the Queen, "it's quite old. And it's the
reason that I've come to you so early on this very special day."

Happily, the Queen led Aurora through the castle to a great portrait hall. It was filled with stately paintings, each of a young princess wearing a crown just like the Queen was wearing.

"Look, Mother! That's you!" exclaimed Aurora, pointing to the nearest portrait.

"Indeed, it is," replied the Queen. It's a tradition in our kingdom that on a princess's seventeenth birthday, this crown is to be passed down to her, to be worn until the day the princess herself becomes queen."

"Oh, Mother!" Aurora gasped. "Is that crown truly to be mine?"

"Well," her mother said with a smile, "I certainly hope so! But you must first earn it by answering three riddles."

Just then, the three good fairies, Flora, Fauna, and Merryweather, flew in.

"Happy birthday, Princess!" said Merryweather. "We're here to give you your clues!"

"Think hard, my dear. And good luck!" the Queen said, turning to leave.

With a wave of their magic wands, the fairies made themselves bigger and transported themselves and Aurora out onto the castle grounds. Then Flora stepped up and recited the first riddle:

"To the eyes, it's a treat; to the nose, a delight.

But beware! To the hand it can be quite a fright.

Though few think to taste it, its sweetness still shows.

To this first riddle, the answer's a _____."

"Hmm . . ." said Aurora when Flora was done.

"Oh! I know!" said Merryweather.

"Of course you know," scolded Fauna. "It's Aurora who has to guess!"

"Do you know what the answer is, dearie?" asked Flora.

"Let's see," said Aurora. "'To the eye, it's a treat.' So it's pretty. 'To the nose, a delight.' So it smells good. 'To the hand . . . quite a fright.' So it must hurt . . . like a thorn on a *rose*! That's it, isn't it?" And she hurried off to the rose garden, where she picked the biggest rose she could find.

"Very good!" exclaimed Fauna. "And now for the second one:

Some plant it, some steal it, some blow it away.
Some do it several times in a day.
Some who are shy might blush getting this
On their hand or their cheek. Can you guess?
It's a _____."

"Well . . ." said Aurora, thinking. "If 'some plant it,' it might be another flower—a dandelion, perhaps? You can blow them away, too. But what can you get on your 'hand' or your 'cheek'?" she wondered aloud as she gazed at her reflection in the garden pool.

"I know!" Aurora cried suddenly. "It's a kiss, isn't it? Of course it is!" And, as if to prove it, she planted a kiss on each of the fairies.

"Honestly," said Flora, "you're figuring out the answers more quickly than any princess yet!"

"Now it's my turn!" exclaimed Merryweather. "Are you ready, Aurora?"

"Yes, I am," she replied.

"Ahem." Merryweather cleared her throat.

"What only gets stronger the longer it lives?

What pays you back tenfold the more that you give?

Some say it's blind, some say it's true,

Some just say simply, 'I feel this for you.'"

Merryweather giggled. "Silly me! I almost said the answer!"

"Let's see," said Aurora. "It might be a tree. That 'gets stronger the longer it lives.' And I suppose you could say that a tree is 'blind.' But so are bats."

Aurora thought and thought. She was still thinking when Prince Phillip walked by.

"Happy birthday, my love!" he called with a big smile.

Instantly, Aurora knew the answer to the third riddle.

Aurora hurried back to the castle and up to her mother's sewing room.

"I've solved the riddles!" she said brightly. She took a pink rose from her hair and handed it to her mother.

"Very good!" declared the Queen. "And the answer to the third riddle?"

That's when the fairies flew in with Prince Phillip.

"It's *love*," said Aurora, "of course!"

No sooner had Aurora said the word than the Queen
took the crown from her head and proudly placed it on
Aurora's. (And then, some say, the heart-shaped diamond
shone even brighter than it had before!)

That night there was a grand birthday ball held in
Aurora's honor.

"Happy birthday, Aurora, my darling," her mother
warmly told her. "And may you have many, many more!"

Cinderella
and the Sapphire Ring

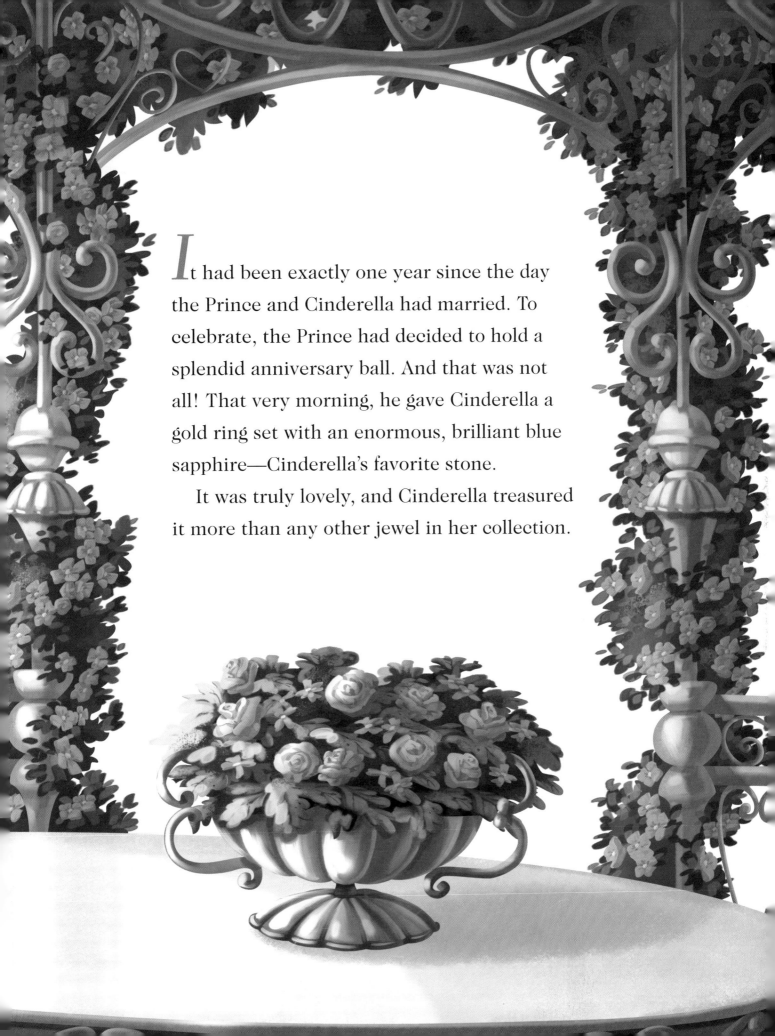

*I*t had been exactly one year since the day the Prince and Cinderella had married. To celebrate, the Prince had decided to hold a splendid anniversary ball. And that was not all! That very morning, he gave Cinderella a gold ring set with an enormous, brilliant blue sapphire—Cinderella's favorite stone.

It was truly lovely, and Cinderella treasured it more than any other jewel in her collection.

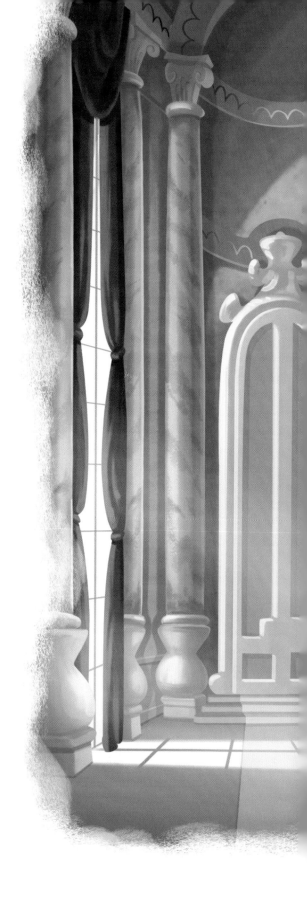

But, alas! The ring was the slightest bit too large . . . and somewhere, sometime over the course of Cinderella's busy day, it had slipped off her left ring finger.

"Oh, no!" cried Cinderella when she looked down and found it gone. "My ring! Where is it?" She quickly checked inside her long gloves, but it was nowhere to be found.

"Don't worry, Cinderelly," her mouse friends Jaq and Gus piped up. "We'll help you find your ring. You can count on us!"

"All we have to do," Jaq declared quite calmly, "is think! Where have you been today?"

Cinderella thought for a moment. "The first thing I did after the Prince gave me the sapphire ring was go back to my bedroom to write about it in my diary."

And so, right away, they hurried to Cinderella's room.

"Do you see it anywhere?" she called to Jaq and Gus.

"No ring," Jaq said with a sigh.

"No ring here, either," sputtered Gus.

"Well, let's try the kitchen, then," said Cinderella brightly. "That's the room I went to next, when I wanted to make a pot of tea."

But the only ring to be found in there was a day-old, sugared donut. "A little stale," said Gus, his mouth full, "but tasty, just the same."

So they hurried on to the music room, where Cinderella had gone to practice a new song.

Jaq and Gus scoured the piano, inside and out. But if the ring was there, they could not find it.

"Perhaps," said Cinderella, "we should try the library. I read there this afternoon."

"To the library!" exclaimed Jaq. "Let's go!"

Although they searched way up high and way down low, they could not find Cinderella's precious sapphire ring in that room, either.

By this time, Cinderella had begun to grow rather nervous. It was nearly time to dress for the anniversary ball! Still, she had not lost hope, and neither had Jaq and Gus.

"You know," Cinderella told them, "I also went out to the stables today to feed and brush dear Frou. So perhaps I lost my ring somewhere in his stall."

The three friends raced to the stable and
searched the stall, sifting through piles and piles of
straw. Gus even searched Frou's feed trough. But
they still had no bright sapphire ring to show for it.

Cinderella scratched her head. "There's only one more place that I can think to look," she said. "The garden, where I went to pick some flowers for the ball."

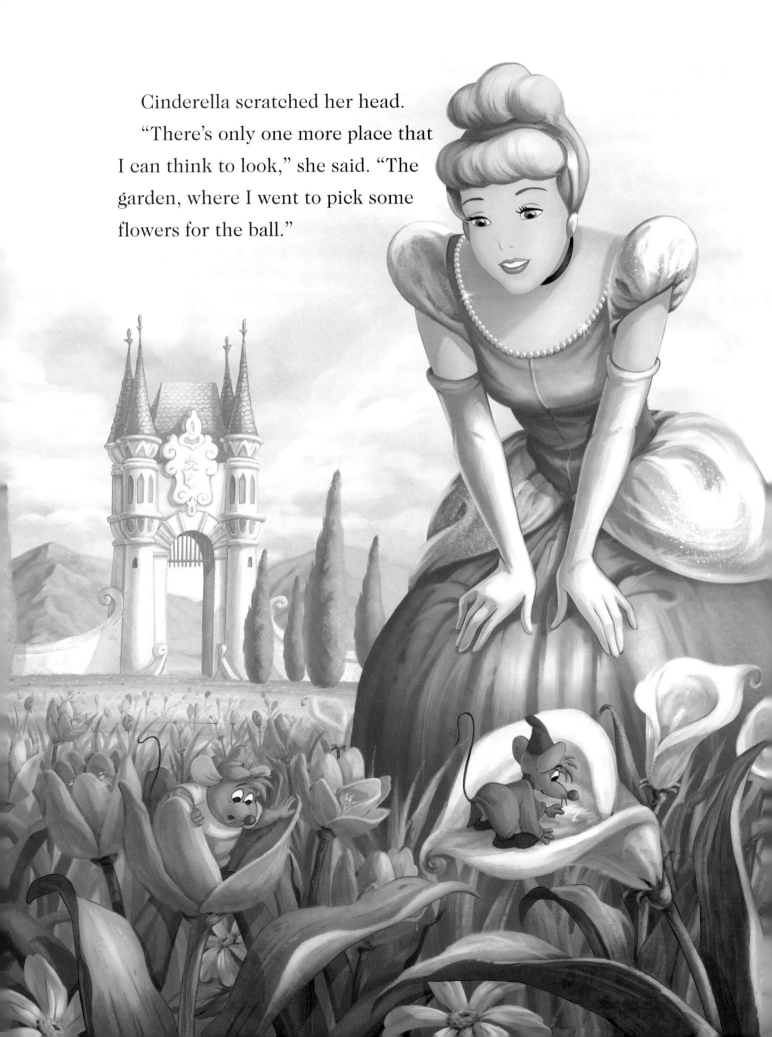

The friends searched each
and every blossom . . . until
Gus exclaimed quite suddenly,
"Cinderelly! I see it!"
He scurried to the ground
and picked up a shiny, round,
blue object.
"Sapphire, Cinderelly?" Gus
asked hopefully.
Cinderella shook her head.
"It's just a marble," she replied.

"Hmm," said Cinderella. "I know my ring is somewhere. But it's late, and I still have to get ready for the ball." She sighed as they walked past the well, back toward the palace.

Then she stopped and turned around.

"Wait a minute. It was after I finished the flower arrangement that I noticed my beautiful ring was gone. And that was just after I drew some water to pour into the vase. You don't suppose," she said, wide-eyed, "it could have fallen down in *there*?"

"I hope not," said Gus, trembling.

But Jaq just rolled his eyes. "Oh, don't be such a scaredy-cat. Get into this bucket!"

"Are you *sure* you want to do this?" Cinderella asked as she slowly lowered Jaq and Gus into the well.

"Of course," Jaq assured her. "It's the only way to see if your ring is down there."

"Do you see anything?" she called down to them several minutes later. "I don't know . . ." said Jaq. "It's pretty dark in here. All I see is lots and lots of—" "*Eek!*"

Cinderella pulled up the bucket as fast as she could, until at last Gus and Jaq were out of the well.

"Thank goodness you're okay!" she cried. "Tell me! What did you poor darlings see?"

"Oh, nothing," said Gus slyly. "Nothing but Cinderelly's ring!"

"My heroes!" cried Cinderella. "You found it! Oh, wait until I tell the Prince how you never gave up until you saved our special day!"

That night at the anniversary ball, the guests toasted the handsome and happily married couple.

Cinderella and the Prince, however, raised their glasses to Gus and Jaq, their guests of honor, and reminded themselves how lucky they were to have such wonderful and devoted little friends.

Jasmine
and the Star of Persia

$\mathcal{P}$rincess Jasmine loved the stars. But even more, she loved the stories Aladdin told her about them. Every night, they would lie on the Magic Carpet and gaze up at the twinkling sky above them.

"What about that star?" Jasmine asked one evening. "The violet one."

"Ah, that," said Aladdin, "is the Star of Persia . . . named after the legendary jewel—the biggest, most beautiful amethyst in the world."

"Jewel?" said Jasmine, her eyes wide with curiosity.

"According to the legend," Aladdin began, "the Star of Persia belonged to a beautiful queen who ruled a tiny kingdom years ago. She was fair and kind. Her subjects loved her dearly, and they lived in happiness and peace for all the years that she reigned.

"When this good queen died," Aladdin continued, "her subjects hid the jewel away, high in a tower, sure that there would never be one worthy of its beauty again."

Jasmine's eyes twinkled. "Tell me, is that story *true*?"

Aladdin shrugged. "I don't know. But there is one way to find out . . . if you really want to."

Jasmine smiled. "Of course I do!"

Early the next morning, Jasmine, Aladdin, and their monkey, Abu, set off on the Magic Carpet. They flew east, and before long, they were soaring over a tiny kingdom. A tall, imposing tower rose from a central plaza.

"Look!" Jasmine called, peering over the edge of the Magic Carpet. "I wonder if that's where the queen's jewel is hidden."

"Let's fly down," said Aladdin. "We'll see if there's a way in."

But when they touched down, they discovered that the tower was completely locked up. It was clear that without a key (or at least a clever genie) there was little chance of getting in.

All of a sudden, the guard standing near the door spoke up. "What do you want?" he demanded.

Jasmine walked up to him. "We've heard about the Star of Persia," she explained, "and we've come to see the jewel."

"That's impossible," the guard said. "If you've heard the legend, you should know that no one can see the jewel except a queen as lovely and worthy as our own."

"Well," said Aladdin, "allow me to introduce you to Princess Jasmine. She's not a queen yet, but she will be one day."

"You couldn't possibly be as fair as our queen," the guard said impatiently.

"I'm very fair," Jasmine assured him.

The guard's eyes searched the plaza. "Fair enough to solve that argument over there?" he asked.

"Yes, I think so." Jasmine nodded. Then she made her way across the plaza and proceeded to do just that.

"You did well," admitted the guard. "But the answer is still no. For our queen was not only fair . . ." He paused for a moment to wipe away a tear. "She was also very kind."

"Ah," said Jasmine, placing her hand on his shoulder. "You still miss her, don't you?" Then she turned to Aladdin. "Let's not bother him anymore," she said. "I'll go get him a drink from that fountain over there. He must get thirsty standing in the sun all day. Then we'll be on our way."

Jasmine hurried to the fountain, which she was
surprised to find quite dry. To her relief, however,
as soon as she held a jar under it, a stream of cool
water came out.

Then, her jar full, she turned to take it to the
guard—only to find him and most everyone else in
the plaza gathered around her, staring.

"What?" she asked. "Did I do something wrong?"

"The fountain!" blurted the guard. "It hasn't given water since our dear queen was alive!

"Many a queen has been fair and kind. But no one else has ever been able to get water from this well." And as the people bowed, the guard drew a key from his pocket.

The guard unlocked the chains barring the tower door. He led Jasmine up a staircase to a room high at the top. There, on a pedestal, sat the gleaming Star of Persia.

"Oh!" Jasmine exclaimed. "It's the most beautiful thing I've ever seen!"

"It is beautiful, isn't it?" said the guard. "And you have proved yourself worthy, Princess Jasmine, to call it your own." And with that, he offered the jewel to Jasmine.

"But how can I ever thank you?" she asked.

"By enjoying it," said the guard, "just as our queen did. Oh! And promise to come visit us whenever you can."

"Oh, I will! I will!" exclaimed Jasmine.
And because she was not only fair
and kind, but honest as well, she most
certainly did.